Delicious and Nutritious

Grow. Eat. Repeat.

A Love Letter to Black-Eyed Peas

Mrs. Mills and her readers,

We hope you love learning about black-eyed peas!

S. Woodson

and
Paige

ISBN: 978-1-7361873-9-5 (Hardcover)
ISBN: 979-8-9856371-0-6 (Paperback)
ISBN: 979-8-9856371-1-3 (E-book)

Illustrations by: Mariana Hnatenko of Nimble Pencils

First printing edition June 2022.

Melanated Magic Books
Phila, PA

www.staceywoodson.com

To our foremothers known and unknown, especially Celia, Marcelena, Doris and Trena, we have the upmost gratitude for all your love and lessons!

– Stacey & Paige

Celia   Doris   Paige

Marcelena   Stacey

This is Paige. Paige spends a lot of time at the community garden, while she's there, she daydreams distractedly about drawing, dancing, or doing gymnastics. These are some of her favorite activities.

Paige's friends often ask her why she agrees to go to the garden since she does not enjoy gardening.

Her answer was short and simple — she loves spending time with her mother. As the oldest child, Paige's mom often invites her to help water and weed the garden. It is one of the few times Paige gets to spend alone with her mother, just the two of them, without her siblings.

Dear Jubilee,

My mom asked me to go to the garden again yesterday. All she talked about was boring facts about plants. First, she explained how the ~~the~~ stem of a plant carries water and nutrients to the leaves. Then, she blabbed about how seeds are living things. She said the inside of every seed contains a baby plant and food for the plant. The bigger the seed, the more food it contains, so you can plant it deeper in the soil. Smaller seeds have less food, so we plant them closer to the surface because the plant will need sunlight to create food more quickly. My mom also explained how people eat different parts of plants. Sometimes, people eat the leaves like greens. Other plants have seeds that are eaten, like ~~beans~~ beans. We eat some plant stalks like celery, and we eat the roots of other plants, ~~such~~ such as beets. I thought that was kind of cool. Maybe our next visit to the garden won't be so boring.

Love, Paige

However, Paige loves having a leisurely lunch on the lawn of the garden while swapping silly stories with her mother.

After enjoying some lavender lemonade, it was time to get to work!

Paige and her mother headed over to the garden, where they admired the growth of their plants. There was a little bit of everything growing in their garden—beans, greens, potatoes, tomatoes; you name it!

"Why do you enjoy gardening so much?" Paige asked her mother.
"Gardening is my way to connect with nature," her mother replied. "It
is also a form of liberation. We will never have to worry about going
hungry as long as we grow our own food."

Paige decided to inspect her strawberries, her favorite plant to grow. She enjoyed watching the strawberries peek out from the little flower petals.

When she heard her mother gasp, Paige ran across the garden to see what had happened.

Her mother was beaming while blissfully looking at a plant.

"What plant is that?" asked Paige.

Paige's mother explained it was her favorite plant—black-eyed peas. The first peas of the season were ready to be harvested!

Paige looked confused. "Why are they called peas?" Paige asked, "They look like beans."

"Great question! You are correct. They are beans. Peas and beans are part of the same family of plants named legumes which grow in pods. There are a few different types of beans referred to as peas. It is confusing," Paige's mother stated with a chuckle.

"Why is this your favorite plant?" Paige inquired. Her mother paused for a second before responding, "Black-eyed peas have a rich history and cultural significance. Our ancestors in Africa loved black-eyed peas so much; that they braided them into their hair. When our ancestors were stolen from Africa, they brought black-eyed peas to America. To know they carried these and other seeds through the Middle Passage is very powerful to me. So, it's an honor to continue their legacy."

"Let me tell you a story about our family," Paige's mother continued. "We come from a long lineage of farmers. However, your Great-Grandmother Marcelena, my grandmother, did not want to carry on the family tradition of farming. When she left Virginia to move up north, she became a seamstress. Years after her mother passed away, she found some black-eyed peas that belonged to her mother.

"Your Great-Grandmother Marcelena felt compelled to plant the seeds that belonged to her mother. She sprinkled the seeds into the soil, and one of the seeds miraculously grew into a plant!

Your Great-Grandmother Marcelena watched as the plant grew, always thinking of her mother. She fell completely in love with gardening when the plant began to bear beans. She was able to nourish herself and even saved some of the black-eyed peas to plant the next season.

Your Great-Grandmother Marcelana taught herself how to grow other plants. She taught all her children to garden, including your Grandmother Doris, my mom, who taught me. The seeds that produced this black-eyed pea plant are called heirloom seeds—or seeds that came from the plants grown by your great-grandmother. These seeds are part of our family history and our journey with generational health."

Fascinated by her family history, Paige couldn't wait to return home to share what she had learned with the rest of her family. While sitting at the dinner table, she told the tale to her father and siblings. Paige's sister and brother were shocked by the story about their great-grandmother. Paige's father shared that his grandmother also grew food.

Paige watched, waited, and worshiped the black-eyed pea plant with wide eyes for the remainder of the growing season. She was determined to learn more about the crop originally from Africa. Paige learned that black-eyed peas provide many nutrients, including potassium, iron, fiber, and protein. She also learned that eating black-eyed peas on New Year's Day is believed to bring prosperity and wealth.

When it came time, Paige was delighted to harvest the black-eyed peas. She collected the peas in a jar and proudly prepared them for her family.

Paige was pleasantly surprised to learn that she could harvest and eat the black-eyed peas, or she could save them to enjoy all year round, even when Mother Earth went into slumber during the winter months.

Paige spent the cold winter months expanding her gardening knowledge. She read books and watched videos about gardening. The following year, she anxiously awaited spring to begin another growing season.

Each year after that, Paige became more passionate about planting food and preserving her family history. She couldn't wait to share her love for black-eyed peas with future generations.

To My Loves,

When I was a child, I thought gardening was boring.
I was about your age when my mother, your Great-
Grandmother Stacey, told me a story about our family
and the cultural significance of black-eyed peas. I fell
madly in love with black-eyed peas and growing food.
Now, I want to share the magic of Mother Earth with
you. These precious heirloom seeds have been in our
family for generations. They have nourished the minds,
bodies, and souls of many of our ancestors. It's time
for you to sow the seeds of generational health for our
descendants. Always remember to nurture Mother Earth,
and she will feed you forever.

Love,

Mom-Mom Paige

About the Authors:

Stacey Woodson, MS, RD, LDN is a dietitian-nutritionist and entrepreneur. She is a counselor, speaker, and author on the topics of nutrition and wellness..

She loves teaching children about healthy eating and introducing them to new foods. She also has a passion for representing and affirming children of color which inspired her to start a clothing line named Melanated Magic Tees. Stacey enjoys gardening, foraging, yoga, and spending time in nature. *Grow. Eat. Repeat. A Love Letter to Black-Eyed Peas* is the second title in the Delicious and Nutritious series. Stacey lives in Philadelphia, PA with her husband, three children, and her cat.

Paige Woodson, is a vibrant 10-year-old who loves gymnastics and art. She also loves to read, garden and frolic in nature. Her favorite foods are tofu and mac-n-cheese. She hopes to travel to Ghana and Paris one day.

View the Delicious & Nutritious Collection

For a complimentary coloring page visit:

www.staceywoodson.com/groweatrepeat

CPSIA information can be obtained
at www.ICGtesting.com
Printed in the USA
BVHW021948191022
649130BV00004B/51